Dear mouse friends,
Welcome to the world of

# Geronimo Stilton

THE RODENT'S GAZETTE
EDITORIAL STAFF

**Geronimo Stilton**
A learned and brainy
mouse; editor of
*The Rodent's Gazette*

**Thea Stilton**
Geronimo's sister and
special correspondent at
*The Rodent's Gazette*

**Trap Stilton**
An awful joker;
Geronimo's cousin and
owner of the store
Cheap Junk for Less

**Benjamin Stilton**
A sweet and loving
nine-year-old mouse;
Geronimo's favorite
nephew

# Geronimo Stilton

## THE STINKY CHEESE VACATION

Scholastic Inc.

ISBN 978-0-545-55631-6

Based on an original idea by Elisabetta Dami.

www.geronimostilton.com

Published by Scholastic Inc., 557 Broadway, New York, NY 10012. SCHOLASTIC and associated logos are trademarks and/or registered trademarks of Scholastic Inc.

*Stilton is the name of a famous English cheese. It is a registered trademark of the Stilton Cheese Makers' Association. For more information, go to www.stiltoncheese.com.*

Text by Geronimo Stilton
Original title *Ma che vacanza... a Rocca Taccagna!*
Cover by Giuseppe Ferrario (design) and Giulia Zaffaroni (color)
Illustrations by Lorenzo De Pretto (design) and Davide Corsi (color)
Graphics by Yuko Egusa

Special thanks to AnnMarie Anderson
Translated by Julia Heim
Interior design by Kay Petronio

12 11 10 9 8 7 6 5 4 3 2 1          14 15 16 17 18 19/0

Printed in the U.S.A.                              40
First printing, May 2014

# A GLOOMY LETTER

It was a **dreary** November evening. A **cold** wind blew, **shaking** the last dry leaves from the branches of the trees that swayed just outside my office window.

## WHAT A GLOOMY ATMOSPHERE!

As the sun **SANK** below the horizon,

Geronimo Stilton's office

long SHADOWS spread over the streets of New Mouse City, the capital of Mouse Island, and the city where I live.

WHOOPS! The gloom must have affected my **manners**, because I forgot to introduce myself. My name is Stilton, *Geronimo Stilton*! I run *The Rodent's Gazette*, the most FAMOUSE newspaper on Mouse Island.

Now where was I? Ah, yes. It was **late** and everyone else on the editorial staff had gone home. But I was still working in my office, which is on the **top** floor of the building. It had been so busy that I still hadn't opened the day's MAIL! I pushed aside a pile of papers and contracts that I needed to read, and I noticed a

letter tied with a gloomy **black** ribbon.

Holey Swiss cheese! It looked like the type of letter someone sends when a mouse has **died**!

My whiskers were **shaking** with worry. With trembling paws, I slowly opened the envelope. Inside, I found a crumpled piece of paper with a **black** border. I glanced at the bottom of the letter to see the signature. It was from SAMUEL S. STINGYSNOUT!

Do you know him? No?! Lucky you!

Samuel Stingysnout is the **stingiest** rodent on Mouse Island. He would do anything to save money or to get his paws on something FREE. And unfortunately Samuel Stingysnout also happens to be . . . my uncle!

I read the letter.

Dear Geronimo,

Excuse the stains on this letter — they are just my sad, sad tears. Dear me, I have some gloomy news: I am informing you of my impending departure from this world (and by this I mean my death, which is coming very, very soon!).

So I beg you to come visit right away. And I mean immediately, or as soon as you possibly can! I am waiting here at Penny Pincher Castle, the Stingysnout family home, to give you my last — and by this I mean my <u>very</u> last — good-bye!

Your affectionate uncle,
Samuel S. Stingysnout

P.S. Don't forget to bring your checkbook!

Oh no! POOR Uncle Stingysnout! Though, when I saw him just a few days ago, he seemed to be in PERFECT health. HOW STRANGE! What could have HAPPENED? He didn't mention anything in the letter. But it was very clear what I needed to do: go and visit him!

Of course, I wasn't sure exactly what I was going to **DO** there (he hadn't mentioned that in the **letter**, either!). But I noticed that he very clearly told me to bring my checkbook. So I put it in my pocket, packed my **suitcase**, and loaded up the car. Then I headed toward Penny Pincher Castle right away!

# THANK GOODMOUSE YOU'RE HERE!

The trip to Penny Pincher Castle was **looooong** and EXHAUSTING. I went through the Valley of Lack (which lacks just about **everything**!) and crossed Loneliness Passage, a remote, little-known gorge. When I reached Scantytown, I finally saw CHEAP CHANGE HILL, the craggy peak where Penny Pincher Castle sits.

I drove up the only street in Scantytown, which has only one lane and clambers up the **mountain**. When I finally arrived at the castle, I couldn't believe my eyes.

**MOLDY MOZZARELLA!** It was so **dilapidated**! It was even worse than the last time I had been there. The castle walls were **crumbling**, the door was unhinged, the windows were all broken, and only a few shingles were left on the **ROOF**. You could tell that my uncle really cared about one thing: saving money!

I tried to ring the doorbell, but it was broken: A spring shot out at me and almost poked me in the **EYE**! When I knocked on the door, one of the last shingles on the roof fell and almost **FLATTENED** me like a pancake!

Yikes!

Outside the Castle

Chimney obstructed by a bird's nest

Precarious eave

Roof with hardly any shingles

Balcony that's about to collapse

Broken windows

Dangling gutters

# Inside the Castle

1. TREASURE ROOM
2. BATHROOM
3. LIVING ROOM
4. BEDROOM
5. UNCLE SAMUEL'S STUDY
6. LIBRARY
7. GREAT HALL
8. BANQUET HALL
9. BEDROOM
10. KITCHEN
11. SITTING ROOM
12. ENTRY HALL
13. BASEMENT
14. GARAGE

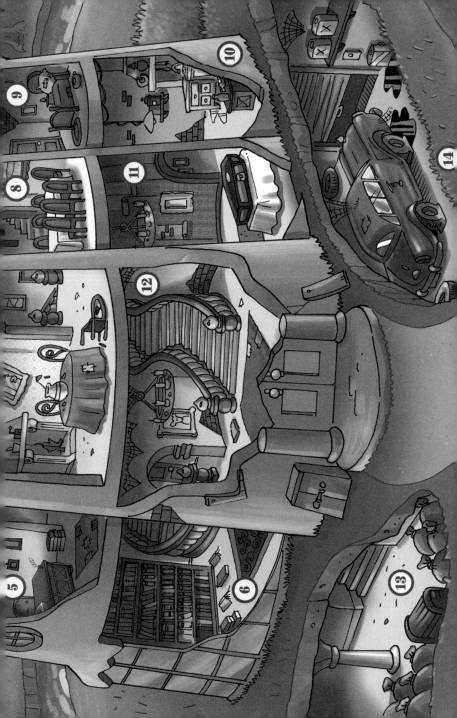

A snout appeared in one of the **broken** windows.

"Come up, **NePHeW**, come up!" a familiar voice squeaked **WEAKLY**. "Thank goodmouse you arrived in time to pay your **last respects**!"

It was a good thing I had arrived there so quickly — **UNCLE STINGYSNOUT** sounded like he was on his last paw! I entered the castle. There was a layer of **DUST** on the furniture, there were spiderwebs everywhere, and it smelled of **mold**. I tried to climb to the second floor, but the stairs were

Ouch!

so **dilapidated** that a plank flew up and smacked me in the snout. *Ouch!*

I finally reached my uncle's room. I found him in bed, **buried** under a pile of blankets. When he saw me, he reached out with a trembling paw.

"Dear nepheeeew," he wheezed. "I am about to leave this world. Waa! Waa! But before I go, I have one last request. I called you because you are my dearest relative, and because all my other relatives **refused**!"

At first, I was **FLATTERED** by my uncle's kind words. After all, my heart is **softer** than mozzarella, and I can be a real cheeseball. But, oh, how I would come to REGRET agreeing to help him!

"What is it, Uncle?" I asked. "Tell me your request, and I promise I'll try to make you happy."

For a moment I thought I saw a **sneaky** look in his eyes.

"Oh, dear nephew, you are so kind and **generous**!" he replied. "I would like my tomb to be in the garden, and I would like it to be surrounded by lots and lots of *flowers*! Can you plant lots of flowers in the castle garden for me?"

"Of course!" I replied. "I'll do it for you *tomorrow*!"

I went to my room feeling **CONTENT**. Tomorrow, I would help grant my uncle's **last request**! But tonight, I would sleep in a room that was incredibly **DRAFTY** because all the windows were broken. Also, the sheets were torn and the blankets were **THIN** and had been **eaten** by moths. Oh, it was going to be a long, **cold** night!

# SINCE YOU'VE ALREADY STARTED . . .

The next morning, I was sleeping soundly when a TREMENDOUS noise woke me with a start.

*Bong!*

I was so **aLaRmeD** I almost jumped out of my fur.

"**WH-WHAT WAS THAT?**" I stammered.

Someone aimed a flashlight right in my eyes, blinding me.

Wh-wh-what . . .

Wh-wh-who . . .

"**AHHHH!**" I squeaked. "Wh-who's there?"

A paw reached out and GRABBED my shoulder.

"**HELP!**" I squealed at the top of my lungs.

It was Uncle Stingysnout.

"Nephew, you really need to **RELAX**!" he said. "You seem very, very **tense** and **nervous**. I just wanted to remind you that the Sun is almost up, so you might want to get out of bed. You should really get moving if you want to plant all the *flowers* before nightfall."

I rubbed my eyes groggily.

"You'll keep your promise, right?" Uncle Stingysnout asked ANXIOUSLY. "You'll plant the garden with lots and lots of flowers before I CROAK, right?"

"Of course, Uncle!" I muttered as I climbed out of bed, still stiff from the COLD night. "I always keep my promises. Rodent's honor."

So I dragged myself to the garden and began planting. Before long, Uncle Stingysnout came to check up on me.

"Since you've already started working, dear nephew, there are a few more things I'd like you to do," he said. "I could use help CUTTING the vines, pulling out the weeds, pruning the trees, watering the lawn, raking the gravel, clearing the pathways, and FERTILIZING the soil. I'd call the gardener, but it costs too much!"

"Oh, all right, Uncle," I agreed with a sigh.

At the end of the day, the garden looked **beautiful**.

"Oh, thank you, Nephew!" Uncle Stingysnout GUSHED dramatically. "Thank you for making the garden so comfortable and flowery. It will be a lovely **eternal** resting place. Sniff, sniff!"

I was so exhausted I barely had the STRENGTH to reply.

"It was nothing, Uncle," I squeaked before I dragged myself to my bed and collapsed. I was so **super-extra-tired** that despite the freezing draft and the constant sound of the shutters banging against my windows, I immediately fell into a *deep*, *deep* sleep.

# SEVEN MORE TEENY, TINY LAST REQUESTS

The next morning I packed my bag and prepared to **HEAD BACK** to New Mouse City. I went to say good-bye to my uncle, but as soon as he saw me holding my suitcase, he started **SOBBING**.

"Oh, thank you for what you did for me, Nephew!" he said. "Go ahead, go back to New Mouse City. Leave me here, **alone and abandoned**. Don't worry about me. I'll be okay. After all, I hardly have any time left. It's not like I have any other **TEENY, tiny** last requests. . . ."

I remembered all the **backbreaking** work I had done in the garden the day before. That had all started out as one **SMALL** request. But because I am a *gentlemouse* (and a good nephew!), I couldn't just leave.

I sighed and put down my suitcase.

"Is there something else I can do for you, Uncle?" I asked.

Uncle Stingysnout JUMPED into the air with joy, as if all his **strength** had suddenly returned.

"Yes!" he squeaked. "Yes, yes, yes, my dear nephew, there are a few more TEENY, tiny things. It's SMALL stuff, really. Just a little something here and there before I go to my cold, DARK, and LONELY grave!"

"That sounds okay," I agreed.

"Actually, it's *seven* little things!" he added *QUICKLY*.

"Seven!" I exclaimed in shock. "Yesterday you told me you had just ONE last request."

He **kneeled** down in front of me.

"Oh, please, please, please, with **cheese** on top?" he begged dramatically. "I don't know what I would do without a **GENEROUS**, **KINDHEARTED** nephew like you!"

"All right, I'll do it," I agreed with a sigh. How could I say **no**?

"Great!" Uncle Stingysnout announced with **satisfaction**. "Here's what I want you to do. . . ."

1 Plant a *flowery* garden around my tomb. (You've already done this one: Good job!)

2 Polish my coffin.

3 FIX my car for the funeral.

4 Find my WILL.

5 Sew my funeral SUIT.

6 Cook DINNER for the funeral.

7 Get the castle ready for the funeral.

# POLISH MY COFFIN, AND THEN . . .

I began polishing my uncle's coffin, but it was falling apart.

"Can you fix it, Nephew?" he asked.

"Of course!" I replied.

I found a hammer and some nails and **repaired** the coffin.

"Erhem." Uncle Stingysnout cleared his throat. "Since you've already started and all the **TOOLS** are out, do you think you might be able to fix this bathroom CABINET, too?"

How could I say NO? So I fixed the bathroom cabinet. Then my uncle asked

me to fix my cousin Stevie's dresser, the cheese cabinet in the kitchen, the bureau in the guest room, the COATRACK in the closet, the green armchairs in the living room, the red chairs in the great hall, the desk in the study, Great-Great-Grandmother Stingysnout's BED, the couch in the storage room, the BOOKSHELVES in the library, the staircase in the hall, the LADDER to the attic, the dining room table, the TABLE near the fireplace, the wood floors in the whole castle, the front DOOR, the small service DOOR, the drawbridge . . . and many, many other things. I did it ALL!

"You see, dear nephew, we couldn't possibly call the carpenter," Uncle Stingysnout explained. "I have to save, save, save, and IT COSTS TOO MUCH!"

Basically, by the end of the day, I had

polished and repaired **ALL** the furniture in the castle!

"Good job, Nephew!" Uncle Stingysnout said, clapping me on the back.

I fell into one of the newly fixed-up armchairs, completely EXHAUSTED. I had terrible blisters all over my paws and

an awful backache. That night I was so tired, I slept like a **WOODEN LOG**. . . . I didn't move an inch!

Good job!

Zzz . . .

# FIX MY CAR, AND THEN . . .

The next morning at dawn, Uncle Stingysnout led me to the **GARAGE**.

"I can't afford a **hearse** for the funeral because **IT COSTS TOO MUCH**!" he told me. "So I'll have to use my own **CAR**. Can you fix it?"

How could I say **no**? So I opened the hood and began to *fiddle* with the pistons, fuses, bolts, and screws. I even got under the car, covering myself completely in **oil**. Finally, after a few hours, I got it running: The car **WORKED PERFECTLY**.

"Erhem." Uncle Stingysnout cleared his throat. "Since you've already started, Nephew, could you fill up the **TANK**, too?"

How could I say **NO**? So I filled up the tank, checked the **pressure** of the tires, and *WASHED*, **waxed**, and **cleaned** the car.

"Since you've already started, Nephew, would you mind fixing the **LAWN MOWER** (it's missing a screw), repairing the **washing machine** (it's clogged with limestone), taking a look at the dishwasher (it makes really strange noises), checking out the **OVEN** (it doesn't heat up properly), repairing the refrigerator (it doesn't get cold), tuning the **television**, and fixing the **RADIO**?" Uncle Stingysnout asked. "You know I can't call the repairman because **IT COSTS TOO MUCH**, right?"

My answer was: **"AAAARGGGHHH!"**
But how could I say **NO**? So I got to
work. Every once in a while, Uncle
Stingysnout came to check on me.

**"Great job!"** he said. "How great you
are, dear nephew!"

I'm sure you can guess what I was like at
the end of the day: completely **exhausted**!
That night I was so **tired**, I slept like a box
of tools. . . . **I didn't move an inch!**
And I did it right there in Uncle Stingysnout's
car!

# FIND MY WILL,
# AND THEN . . .

The next morning I woke up feeling tired but happy: Today's task would be an **EASY** one! All I had to do was find Uncle Stingysnout's will.

My uncle was waiting for me in the library, where he greeted me with a **suspicious**-looking smile.

"Good morning, dear nephew," he said. "Today you have to find my will. I think it's hidden somewhere in this library, in one of these seven thousand books!"

I almost *fainted* when I looked UP at the ROWS AND ROWS of books. They never seemed to end! But how could I say **no**? So I rolled up my sleeves and began to sift through the books **ONE BY ONE**.

"**Erhem**." Uncle Stingysnout cleared his throat. "Since you've already started, could you also organize these books alphabetically? And dust them off, **ONE BY ONE**? You know, no one has cleaned in here for about twenty years. I can't hire a cleaner because **IT COSTS TOO MUCH**!"

How could I say **NO**? I got to work, but in order to get to the books on the **TOP** shelves, I needed a ladder. I found the

Sigh!

TALLEST one in the castle. But as I was climbing, a rung broke and I fell ❶. I landed on a wooden desk ❷, then I tumbled to the floor, massaging my head where a great big BUMP had formed ❸. Suddenly, I noticed something strange ❹. Falling onto the desk had activated a HIDDEN mechanism that was linked to a SECRET drawer. The drawer had opened, and inside was a rolled-up SCROLL! I grabbed the scroll and ran to find Uncle Stingysnout ❺.

"Uncle, I think I found your will!" I squeaked.

Uncle Stingysnout grabbed the scroll and stuffed it in his pocket.

"No, no," he said quickly. "It's not my will, UNFORTUNATELY."

So I got back to work searching for

the will among all those books while I **alphabetized** and dusted.

I had just finished dusting the library when my uncle POPPEd into the room again.

"Erhem," he said, clearing his throat. "Since you've already started, would you mind dusting the **ENTIRE CASTLE**, from the ground floor to the attic?"

How could I say **NO**? So I dusted the **ENTIRE CASTLE** (and I mean the **WHOLe** thing!), but I still hadn't found the will **ANYWHERE**! Just as I was about to find my uncle to explain the situation, he suddenly appeared, **rustling** a piece of paper.

"Nephew, have you finished already?" he asked. "**You're so great!** And I have good news: I found my will! It was in my safe the whole time. How **Silly** of me to have **forgotten**!"

Here it is!

"Oh, I'm so happy!" I managed to stutter before I passed out from EXHAUSTioN. That night, I was so tired I slept like a stack of books. . . . I didn't move an inch! And in my dreams, I was chased by hundreds of dusty dictionaries!

# SEW MY FUNERAL
# SUIT, AND THEN . . .

The next morning, I was so **tired** I had trouble getting up. But I had work to do — I needed to patch up Uncle Stingysnout's funeral suit. I'll admit it: I'm not very good at sewing. But I promised myself I would try my BEST for poor Uncle Stingysnout.

I sat down in a chair and opened the WOODEN box that contained the needles, thread, scissors, and thimble. I was having a really hard time THREADING the needle when I stabbed myself in the paw. **Ouchie!** After a few more attempts, I finally got it. My uncle's suit was full of holes and PATCHES, but after a few hours, I was finished.

I sighed with relief.

"Uncle Stingysnout, I'm finished!" I yelled.

He came quickly. "Already?" he asked. "How great! Since you've already started and you have some extra time on your paws, could you patch my underwear, socks, undershirts, shirts, ties, jackets, pants, and handkerchiefs? And then maybe mend the castle sheets, towels, dishcloths, and aprons?"

I'll do it!

I was about to have a **PANIC** attack, but how could I say **NO**? I gathered my STRENGTH and grabbed my needle.

"Okay, okay, Uncle," I said. "I'll mend it **all** — every last **THING**!"

By afternoon, I was almost finished. But then Uncle Stingysnout arrived with a pile of cotton, linen, and velvet **fabric** in all different **colors**. "Since you've already started, can you reupholster the LOVE SEAT in the entryway, the sofa in the living

Hee, hee, hee!

room, the chair in the pantry, the chair in the study, and all the FURNITURE in the castle?" he asked. "And can you sew some nice new CURTAINS that will cover the windows of the castle? And sew some new BEDSPREADS for all the bedrooms? I would hire a seamstress, but IT COSTS TOO MUCH!"

When I was finally done I was so TIRED I fell asleep in a laundry basket. That night I slept like a pile of laundry. . . . I didn't move an inch!

# COOK DINNER
## FOR THE FUNERAL,
## AND THEN . . .

The next morning, I woke up to find Uncle Stingysnout standing over me with an **APRON** and a **CHEF'S HAT**.

"Dearest Geronimo," he said. "You'd better get up and put these on. After all, today you have to cook for my **FUNERAL** banquet! You understand why I can't hire a chef, right? **IT COSTS TOO MUCH!**"

I sighed and dragged my tail out of bed. Then I headed to the kitchen.

When I saw the list of all the different **foods** my uncle wanted

me to prepare, I was SQUEAKLESS. It was more food than any mouse could eat in an entire year!

But how could I say **no**? I immediately ran off to do the shopping. I bought more food than I could **CARRY**! Finally, I began to cook. I made tons of teeny, tiny appetizers, enormouse trays of lasagna, dozens of roasts, **mountains** of cheese cubes, plates and plates of vegetables, and **HUNDRED$** of pies and cheesecakes.

Ugh!

Cheesecake is definitely my specialty.

"Keep on **COOKING**, Geronimo!" Uncle Stingysnout urged me. "Make **LOTS AND LOTS** of food because we don't know how much we'll **need**! Who knows? Hundreds of people will probably show up for my **FUNERAL**!"

It was late at night by the time I was finished **COOKING**, cleaning up the

Cook more, Nephew!

kitchen, and washing all those **dirty** pots and pans. I put all the food in Uncle Stingysnout's enormouse **freezer**.

When Uncle Stingysnout came to **CHECK UP** on me, he opened the freezer and **TEARS** of joy filled his eyes. He was so **GLAD** to see all that precooked food ready to be **defrosted** that I was proud I had helped make his last days **HAPPY** ones.

"I'm finished, Uncle," I muttered, exhausted.

*Perfect!*

"Can I go to **SLEEP** now?"

"Great job, Nephew!" he exclaimed, patting my back with his paw. "Yes, yes. Go to **BED**. You'll need your rest, because tomorrow will be a **VERY** hard day. . . ."

But I wasn't listening to him anymore. Instead, I was sleeping while standing up, leaning against the **ENORMOUSE** freezer, a dish towel still in my paw!

That night, I was so tired I slept like an **overstuffed** turkey. . . .

I didn't move an inch!

# GET THE CASTLE READY . . . AND THAT'S IT!

The next morning when I **WOKE UP** I was still leaning against the freezer.

"Good **morning**, Nephew!" Uncle Stingysnout squeaked happily. "Today, you will fulfill my very **LAST** wish: get Penny Pincher Castle ready for the **FUNERAL**! But it might take more than a **DAY** to do it. . . ."

I was *worried*. "What exactly do you mean by '**GET THE CASTLE READY**'?" I asked.

"Erhem, well . . ." he said, **CLEARING** his throat and pulling out a very LOOOONG list. "My dearest nephew, this is what I mean

by '**GET THE CASTLE READY**': paint the walls and ceilings, **WAX** the floors, **REDO** the electrical system, **repair** the plumbing, clean the sewers, **RESTORE** the roof, **install** heating and air-conditioning, and **transform** the pond into a heated swimming pool! I wish I could hire a contractor to do it, but as you know, dear nephew, **IT COSTS TOO MUCH!**"

I couldn't take it anymore! I took one look at the list and I **FAINTED**.

It costs too much!

A **MOMENT** later, Uncle Stingysnout awakened me with a bucket of **ice-cold** water in the snout.

"**Wake up**, Geronimo!" he squeaked. "I'm counting on you to refurbish the castle INSIDE AND OUT. And when I say INSIDE AND OUT, I really mean **INSIDE AND OUT**. This is my very **Last** request!"

"B-but, Uncle —" I began, but he cut me off.

Wake up!

"Oh, poor, poor me!" he moaned. "I'm so **old** and so **sick**, and I just have this one †iNY last request before I croak, which might be **very, very** soon! You'll help me out, won't you, Nephew?"

MOLDY MOZZARELLA! This time, I knew I couldn't do it **alone**. It was too much WORK! It would take me an entire year to refurbish the castle inside and out. There was only one thing to do. . . .

# WE'RE HERE TO HELP!

I had no choice: I had to ask for **HELP**! So I got on the *phone* and called my relatives and all of my friends. A few hours later, a **FLOOD** of rodents arrived.

It was my entire family: my sister, THEA; my cousin TRAP; my beloved nephew BENJAMIN; and even Grandfather William Shortpaws. Tina Spicytail, Aunt Sweetfur, Uncle Grayfur, Aunt Sugarfur, Uncle Kindpaws, Squeaky and Squeakette, Grandma Rose, and Grandpa Hayfur were all there, too!

After my family arrived, my *friends* and coworkers from *The Rodent's Gazette* followed: my charming friend Petunia Pretty Paws, my adventurous friend Wild

**Willie** and his adventurous cousin Maya, my athletic friend **BRUCE HYENA**, and my detective friend HERCULE POIRAT were all there, along with many others!

Everyone gathered around me.

"What do you **need**, Geronimo?" someone asked.

"Yeah, we're here to **HELP**!"

I told them about the letter I had received from Uncle Stingysnout, and about how I had promised my poor uncle that I would fulfill his seven FiNaL requests. Then I explained how I was neVeR going to be able to keep my promise.

The crowd was totally SILENT. Finally, my sister, Thea, squeaked up.

"Friends, I don't know if you know Samuel S. Stingysnout . . ." she began.

"Of course we do!" someone replied. "He's

the **stingiest** rodent on Mouse Island!"

"Forget Mouse Island," Trap added. "I think he might win champion of the **WORLD**!"

"It's true!" little Benjamin squeaked in agreement. "Uncle Stingysnout is a real **CHEAPSKATE**!"

"I don't think Uncle Stingysnout is really sick," Thea grumbled. "I think he's **FAKING** it!"

"I'm not surprised he called *you*, Geronimo," Trap taunted me. "You would believe anything!"

But Benjamin defended me.

"No, Uncle G just has a heart of **GOLD**," Benjamin explained. "It's as **soft and tender** as a ball of mozzarella!"

I was **shocked** and upset. "But why would Uncle Stingysnout fake a terrible illness?" I squeaked.

# UNCLE STINGYSNOUT, THE CHEAPEST RODENT ON MOUSE ISLAND!

He washes his hands with barely any soap so it doesn't get used up!

When he makes tea, he reuses the same tea bag over and over again!

When it rains, he doesn't use an umbrella. He saves water because he doesn't shower that day!

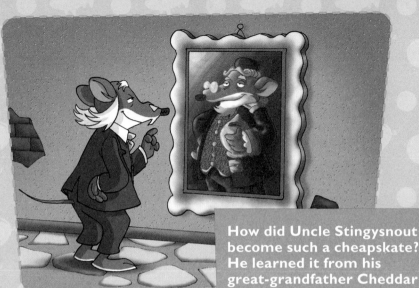

How did Uncle Stingysnout become such a cheapskate? He learned it from his great-grandfather Cheddar Cheapskate, who barely ever spoke because he was always saving his breath!

He painted flames on the fireplace so he wouldn't have to buy wood!

He reads by the light of lightning to save money on his electric bill!

WE'RE HERE  TO HELP!

"What a **rotten** thing to do! I don't believe it."

Everyone was **quiet**.

"You don't have to **HELP** me," I told my friends and family. "But I'm not leaving. I made a **PROMISE** to my uncle, and I'll stay here until it's done, even if it takes me an entire year to **FIX UP** the castle."

"Don't worry, Uncle G," Benjamin piped up. "I'll stay."

"Me too," Thea agreed.

"We all still think Uncle Stingysnout is being a **trickster**, but we'll stay to help you, **Geronimo**!" Trap added. Other mice around him nodded in agreement.

"**THANK YOU, FRIENDS!**" I replied, relieved.

Everyone got to work **RIGHT AWAY**. Still, it took an entire week to **restore** the castle.

Each mouse worked on a specific task, depending on his or her **SKILLS**. For

example, Hercule Poirat is a detective, so he worked on installing the **ALARM** system.

Bruce Hyena is a very adventurous mouse who isn't afraid of heights (or anything else, for that matter). So he fixed the **SHINGLES** on the roof. Grandpa Shortpaws is a FORMIDABLE organizer, and he made sure everyone was on schedule. Aunt Sweetfur is a great decorator, so she made sure the castle furniture and décor looked amazing.

Everyone worked together, and we had **FUN** while we got the job done! When we were finished, the castle looked totally different than it had when we started. Turn the page to see the "**before**" and "**after**" for yourself!

# HEY YOU, PORTER!

I was truly **satisfied** with the end result. The work had been very **HARD**, but it had been worth it. After all, I made my sick uncle **HAPPY** and saved the Stingysnout family name!

Most of my family and friends had gone **HOME**, but Thea, Trap, Benjamin, and I remained. We were packing up our things to head back to New Mouse City when the door **BURST** open. A tall, **MUSCULAR**, rodent strode into the castle. He was wearing a very *elegant* suit, and he was carrying a designer suitcase.

"Hey you, **porter**," he squeaked rudely. "I have a *reservation* for tonight! Here's my bag." He handed me his suitcase.

"I'm sorry, sir," I replied courteously. "But you must be mistaken. This is a private home, not a **hotel**."

"No, no, no!" he insisted. "You're the mouse who's **MISTAKEN**. This *is* a hotel: *Hotel Stingysnout*! And it's top-notch, too. It's a five-cheese resort!"

He handed me a tiny coin.

"This is for you," he said. "It's a **tip**!"

I tried to object, but he had already turned around to call to someone behind him.

"Come, come, my *dear*," he said. "Our **ROOM** will be ready in a minute."

He **GLARED** at me intently as a blonde rodent dressed in the latest style entered the castle, her tall heels CLICK-CLACKING on the newly restored marble floor. I recognized her immediately: It was **Faith**

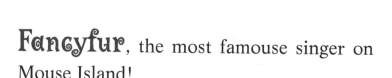
**Fancyfur**, the most famouse singer on Mouse Island!

"Ooh!" she squeaked. "This hotel is so **cute**! The pool's heated, right? And where's the cook? I want some **CHEESECAKE** right away. I'm as **hungry** as a cat!"

"Um, yes, miss, the pool is heated," I replied instinctively. "But this isn't a hotel. **I'M SORRY!**"

"Hey, no more **JOKES**," the burly mouse protested angrily. "We have a reservation to spend the weekend here at *Hotel Stingysnout*. Now get the room ready before I **LOSE** my patience! And bring us two slices of cheesecake, **PRONTO**! I hear it's the hotel *specialty*."

Right at that moment Thea, Trap, and Benjamin arrived. They were carrying a stack of colored *flyers* with the words HOTEL STINGYSNOUT typed in **BIG** letters.

"Hey, Geronimo, look what we found!" Trap said.

# HOTEL STINGYSNOUT?

I read the flyer, but I had **TROUBLE** believing it:

★ ★ ★ ★ ★ ★ ★ ★ ★ ★ ★ ★ ★ ★ ★ ★ ★ ★ ★ ★ ★ ★ ★ ★

## Hotel Stingysnout

FIVE-CHEESE RESORT!

NEWLY RENOVATED!

FEATURES A BEAUTIFUL GARDEN

AND A HEATED POOL!

★ ★ ★ ★ ★ ★ ★ ★ ★ ★ ★ ★ ★ ★ ★ ★ ★ ★ ★ ★ ★ ★ ★ ★

My phone buzzed, and I received an automatic text-message advertisement. I read it, **shocked**:

Come to Hotel Stingysnout! It's the most fashionable new hotel on Mouse Island!

A second later, my phone buzzed again! This time it was a phone call from my friend Priscilla Prettywhiskers.

"Hi, Geronimo!" she said. "I just heard that your uncle Samuel Stingysnout transformed his castle into a fantastic new hotel! It's supposed to be very exclusive, and I hear cheesecake is the house specialty! Do you think there are rooms available for this weekend?"

As I was listening to Priscilla, Uncle Stingysnout **BOUNCED** down the stairs, looking **healthy**.

"Welcome, dear guests!" he announced GAILY. "Welcome to the FaBUMOUSe Hotel Stingysnout! Allow me to give you a tour of this new, incredibly comfortable hotel! We even have a HEATED pool!"

**Moldy mozzarella!** He didn't even seem **SICK** anymore! Bewildered, I turned to my uncle.

"H-hotel Stingysnout?" I stammered. "B-but what does this **mean**?"

As soon as he saw Trap, Thea, Benjamin, and me, Uncle Stingysnout **STOOPED OVER** and grabbed his back, **COUGHING** dramatically.

A second later, Uncle Stingysnout saw the two **TOURISTS** and the stack of colored flyers Trap was holding. He straightened himself up and sighed.

"At this point, I guess you figured out everything, **RIGHT**?" he asked.

"Yes, Uncle, we know," I squeaked, my paws on my hips. "But I'd still like an **explanation**!"

I was so **ANGRY** and upset with him!
"I'll tell you all the TRUTH, the whole
TRUTH, and nothing but the TRUTH!" he
agreed with a sigh. "You see, I wanted to
open a hotel in the castle, but the building
was falling to PIECES, and I
needed so many new things,
like a *beautiful* garden and a
heated pool! But I didn't want
to spend any **MONEY**. So I
thought of asking Geronimo for
help. He's so kind, and he never
says no to anyone. . . ."

I can't say no!

Everyone looked at me. I knew what they
were thinking: that I'm a softhearted
mouse who will believe ANYTHING! And
it's true — I really am like that. If someone
asks me for **HELP**, I can't say no. But is
that such a **bad** thing?

"So, as I was saying," Uncle Stingysnout continued, "I thought I would ask Geronimo for help. I invented the excuse that I was sick and was about to **CROAK**, and that I had seven **FINAL** requests."

Thea shook her head.

"You should be ashamed of yourself, Uncle Stingysnout," she said. "You took advantage of Geronimo's *good faith* in you."

"Yeah!" Trap agreed. "Double shame on you, for all the lies you told and for being such a **PENNY PINCHER**!"

Uncle Stingysnout hung his head. "I realize now it was wrong," he said. "*I'm so sorry!*"

Benjamin didn't say a thing, but I saw that he was sad.

"Uncle Stingysnout, I'm hurt because you **tricked** everyone," he said finally. "But I love you and I **FORGIVE** you."

He gave Uncle Stingysnout a **huge** hug. Uncle Stingynout **hugged** him back, crying.

"Thank you, Benjamin," he **SOBBED**. "I **PROMISE** I won't do it again!"

He turned to me.

"How about you, Geronimo?" he asked remorsefully. "Do you **forgive** me?"

I sighed. I was still UPSET with him, but I love my uncle, despite his *flaws*!

"Of course I do!" I replied.

"Let's go and have a SWIM together in the heated pool," Benjamin suggested, taking Uncle Stingysnout's paw.

"Great idea!" Uncle Stingysnout replied. "Then we'll have a cheesecake party: The freezer is full! We'll eat together — all FIVE of us! What do you say?"

"Let's do it!" Benjamin replied happily.

# SHOW US THE MAP!

We stayed another day in the castle, sharing the cheesecake and the pool with the guests of Hotel Stingysnout!

The next morning we were ready to **LEAVE**. We went to say good-bye to Uncle Stingysnout and found him seated behind the **DESK** in the library of the castle — I mean, the hotel. I noticed that he seemed very SAD.

"What's wrong, Uncle?" I asked.

He sighed. "**NOTHING**, Nephew."

So Benjamin approached him.

"You can tell me," he said. "Why aren't you **HAPPY**?"

Uncle Stingysnout began to **CRY**, but he wouldn't say **WHY**.

"Come on," Thea insisted. "Tell us what's wrong, Uncle!"

"Yeah," Trap added. "But tell us the **truth** this time!"

Uncle Stingysnout dried his tears on my jacket and BLEW his nose on my tie. (To save money, he never kept tissues in his pocket.)

"It all started when Geronimo found that

**SCROLL**!" he moaned.

"Geronimo!" Thea scolded. "What have you done now?"

"I haven't done **anything**!" I protested. "What scroll, Uncle? And why is everything always my **fault**!?"

Uncle Stingysnout continued to **SOB**. "As I was saying, that scroll was actually a **MAP**. . . ."

"A map?" we all shouted.

"What kind of **MAP**?" Trap squeaked.

Uncle Stingysnout clutched the scroll to his chest, **kissing** it and **cuddling** it.

"It's a **TREASURE** map!" he sobbed.

His words echoed through the castle:

*Treasure!!! Treasure!!! Treasure!*

"I need your **HELP** finding the treasure,"

he continued between sobs. "But I don't know how to ask you! Of course now you won't want to help me anymore, after I **TRICKED** all of you."

Suddenly, my **detective** friend Hercule Poirat popped out from behind a column.

"Oh, for a **tHOUSanD** bananas!" he exclaimed. "Did I hear the word *treasure*? Please allow me to be of service! I am the **best** detective in New Mouse City!"

"Thank you, Hercule," I replied. "That's very **kind** of you. Now let's not waste any more time. Show us the **Map**, Uncle!"

"Yeah!" Thea exclaimed. "Let's see it! We'll search for the treasure **TOGETHER**, and then we'll split it into **equal** parts."

Uncle Stingysnout **SQUINTED** at us **suspiciously**.

"What if you take the **treasure** and keep it for yourselves?" he asked.

I shook my head at him indignantly.

"We would never do something like that!" I protested. "We're **honest** rodents, Uncle!"

"You, on the other hand . . ." Trap **mumbled** under his breath.

"How dare you?!" Uncle Stingysnout cried. "Are you saying that I would **STEAL** the treasure from all of you?"

"Well, you *are* a real **CHEAPSKATE**," Benjamin remarked candidly.

"And you don't have the greatest track record when it comes to **honesty**," Trap added.

"That's enough!" I squeaked. "Let's shake paws and **promise** to help each other. Then we can start **LOOKING** for this treasure!"

"Okay, okay," Uncle Stingysnout agreed. "I promise not to steal any of the treasure, **StiNGYSNOUt'S HONOR**!"

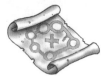

# THE TREASURE HUNT

Uncle Stingysnout finally showed us the map.

"The **MAP** says that we have to **EXPLORE** the castle from top to bottom," Benjamin pointed out.

"It also says the treasure is 'At the bottom of the bottom,'" Thea added. "But who knows what that means."

Hercule examined the map.

"Hmm, this map seems very **old**, doesn't it?" he observed. Then he held the map up to his snout and took a big sniff. "And it smells very **STRANGE**, too . . . like **STINKY** old cheese!"

"Geronimo, did you notice anything **interesting** while we were doing all that

IF IT'S THE TREASURE YOU WANT TO DISCOVER,

FROM TOP TO BOTTOM YOU MUST UNCOVER

THE SYMBOL OF CHEESE, WHEREVER IT LIES.

LOOK CAREFULLY, FOR IT'S DISGUISED!

AND IF THE TREASURE YOU CAN'T SEEM TO FIND,

KEEP SNIFFING IT OUT, LIKE AN OLD CHEESE RIND!

YOU'LL LOCATE IT SOON IF YOU LOOK AROUND,

AT THE BOTTOM OF THE BOTTOM IS WHERE IT'S FOUND!

WORK on the castle?" Hercule asked me.

I shook my head.

"No, nothing!" I replied. "I was too busy dusting and cleaning the castle from top to bottom, from the FIRST FLOOR to the ATTIC!"

"From the first floor to the attic?" Hercule repeated. "Hmm . . . but the first floor isn't the bottom of the castle, is it? Uncle Stingysnout, what is beneath the first floor?"

Uncle Stingysnout JUMPED out of his chair.

"Why, the CELLAR is under the first floor!" he cried. "But no one has been DOWN there in years. It's dark, and we'd have to WASTE candles to see!"

"Come on, Uncle!" we all shouted. "Don't be so cheap!"

We scrounged around and found five candle stubs with extensions. Uncle Stingysnout had iNVeNteD them to save money!

A CANDLE STUB WITH AN EXTENSION . . .
TO SAVE MONEY!

We LIT our candles and *descended* the worn-out staircase that led to the castle's cellar. Uncle Stingysnout stayed upstairs to wait for us so he wouldn't waste any energy searching for the treasure. He really is the STINGIEST mouse in the world!

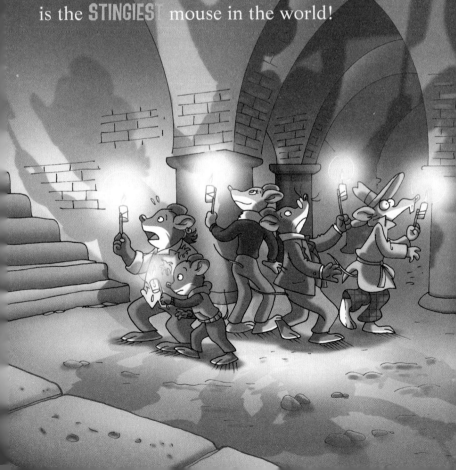

As we were going down the stairs, Trap couldn't stop chattering.

"I bet the treasure will be enormouse!" Trap said, his eyes sparkling. "After all, the Stingysnouts are so **CHEAP**, they never spend anything! So they've probably been building up a treasure for years!"

We searched the basement for HOURS and HOURS, but we didn't find a thing.

"Oh, I'm getting so **HUNGRY**!" Hercule complained. "I'm as hungry as a cat from all this searching. Does anyone have a **BANANA**?"

No one did. We looked and looked for the treasure as our candle stubs burned low. As the light dimmed, the SHADOWS on the walls of the cellar grew **LONGER** and **SCARIER**.

"Wh-what was that?" I squeaked, my whiskers trembling with fright. A dark shadow had just JUMPED out at me.

"It's just me, Uncle," Benjamin said sweetly, lowering the paw that held his candle, which was DRIPPING wax all over the cellar floor.

I sighed with relief. I thought it had been a GHOST!

Hercule hung his head dejectedly as we continued to search for the CHEESE symbol the map mentioned.

"Maybe I was **wrong**," he muttered to himself. "Maybe the treasure isn't in the cellar after all."

# THE BOTTOM OF THE BOTTOM

I looked at the map again carefully and tried to **CONSOLE** Hercule.

"It's very **STRANGE**," I told him. "I also thought the treasure would be here in the cellar. We can't get any closer to the **BOTTOM** than this!"

Poor Hercule just shook his head dismally.

"It doesn't seem like it is," he admitted. "For a thousand bananas, the map **fooled** us all!"

Feeling defeated, we began to climb **up** the **stone** steps that led out of the cellar.

We were halfway up the stairs when Benjamin turned **around** for a moment.

"**LOOK!**" he shouted suddenly.

# "THERE IT IS!"

I turned around, my heart **racing** with excitement. There it was: the symbol of the CHEESE WEDGE!

There it is!

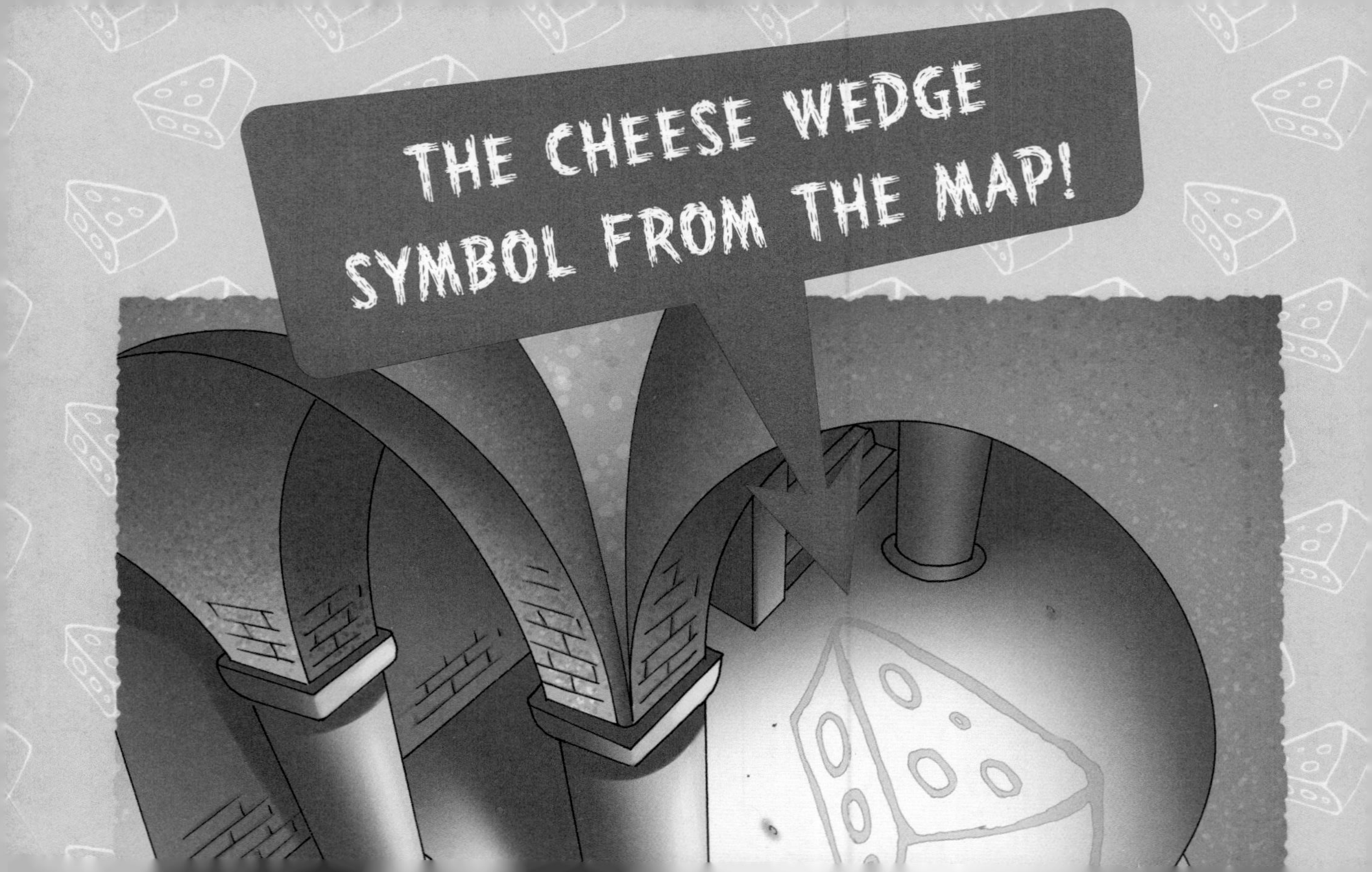
THE CHEESE WEDGE
SYMBOL FROM THE MAP!

It was carved into the stone floor of the cellar, which is why the map had said it was at "the bottom of the bottom"! That's also why we hadn't seen it before: It was only visible when we were standing on the staircase **ABOVE** the floor!

We *DASHED* back down the steps, **GRABBED** some shovels that were propped in a corner of the basement, and immediately began **DIGGING**. The floor was made of small **stones**, and we lifted them up one at a time. It was **INCREDIBLY** exhausting! Even though they were tiny, they were so, so **heavy**. It took many hours of hard work to remove them all!

Trap directed us while we worked. "**Lift it out! Dig it in! Pick it up!** Come on!" he squeaked. "Keep it up!"

In reality, Trap was taking advantage of

the situation (as usual). While we worked hard, he was doing **nothing**! Still, we continued to **dig** and **dig** and **dig**.

Then, suddenly, Thea's shovel **HIT** something. We finally discovered what was beneath the cellar floor. There, at the very "bottom of the bottom," was a **wooden** chest decorated with brass studs!

Hercule hoisted it up and popped the lid open **easily**. We gasped.

Immediately, the irresistible smell of **aged cheese** rose from the chest! Inside were ten perfectly identical wheels of vintage cheese. Each wheel had the date 1313 stamped on it, along with the name of the cheese: Truffled Cheddar (Extra-Stinky).

We couldn't believe our **LUCK**! The chest of cheese was a **PRICELESS** treasure!

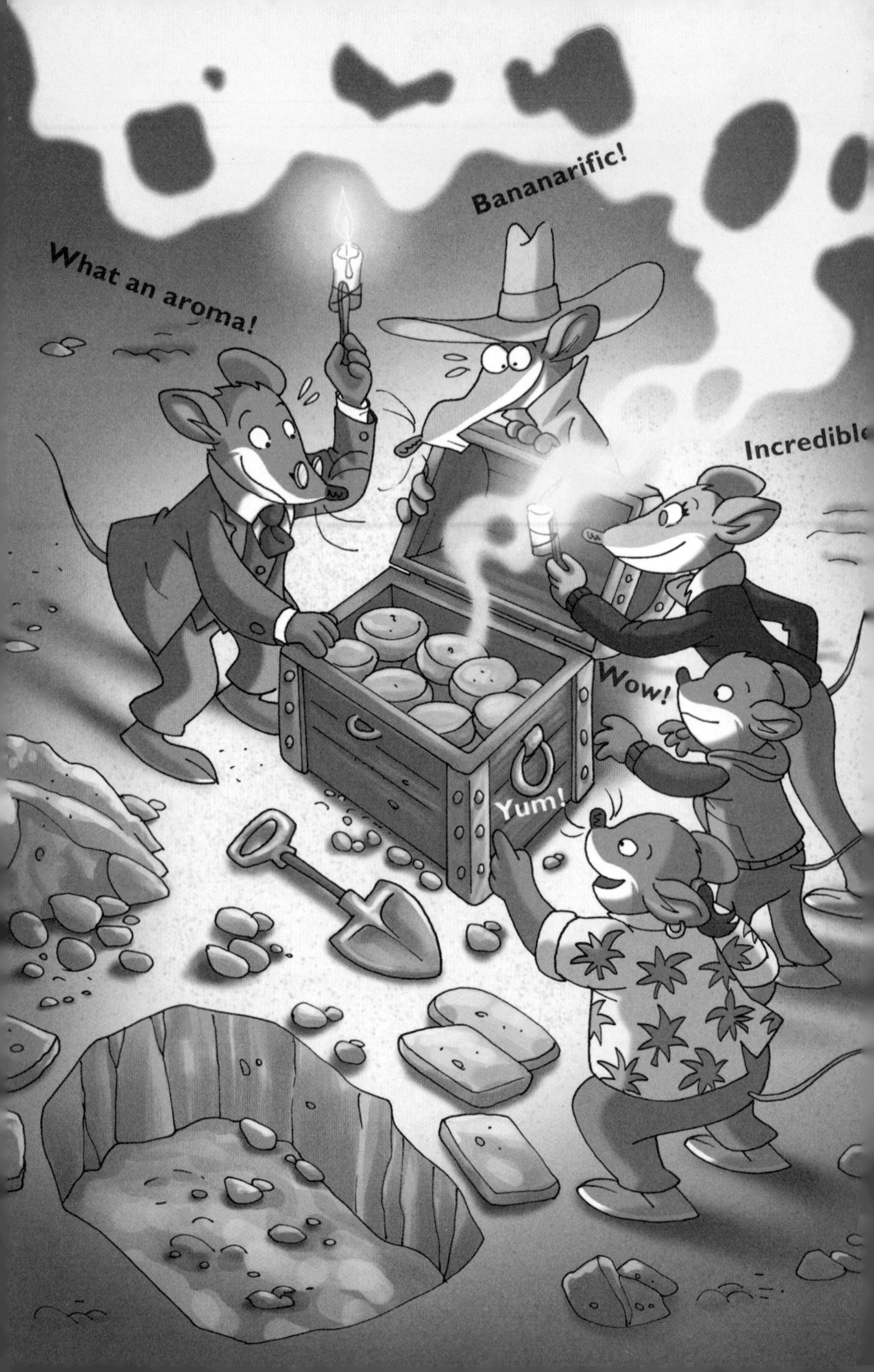
What an aroma!
Bananarific!
Incredible
Wow!
Yum!

# A STINKY TREASURE

We carried the **HEAVY** chest back up the stairs that led out of the cellar and into the castle. Uncle Stingysnout was waiting for us at the TOP of the stairs, **eager** to see what we had found.

"So, did you find it?" he asked **impatiently**. "Huh? Huh? Where's **MY** — er, I mean, *our* treasure?"

"**Patience**, patience," Hercule said as we placed the chest down and opened the lid. The intense aroma

Where is it?

of cheese filled the air around us immediately.

"Mmm," Hercule said. "Now that we've done all the hard work **digging up** this chest, I think it's time for a YUMMY little snack!"

Uncle Stingysnout's eyes lit up when he saw the chest.

"OHHHHHHHHHHHHHH!"

he exclaimed. "It's a chest full of precious aged cheese!"

He held out his paw.

"Here, give me the treasure," he said. "I'll divide it up: one cheese for everyone to share, and I'll keep the other nine."

Hercule snapped the chest shut.

"NO, NO, NO," he scolded Uncle Stingysnout. "That wasn't the agreement! Are you trying to steal everyone else's treasure?"

Hercule opened the chest again and removed one wheel of cheese. He brought it up to his mouth and pretended to take a bite.

"Oh, oh, oh, I'm so HUNGRY!" Hercule said. "Since the deal is off, I think I'll just eat all this cheese right now. Yum, yum, yum!"

Suddenly, Uncle Stingysnout looked SCARED. He believed Hercule was going to eat up all that cheese — right then and there!

"Wait, wait!" Uncle Stingysnout cried. "I'm sorry! I accept your conditions for dividing up the cheese, just please don't EAT any of it!"

We divided up the cheese eQuaLLy. Uncle Stingysnout quickly locked his cheese up in his SAFE. We packed our cheese into our luggage and finally headed **home** to New Mouse City.

# A FREE VACATION!

In New Mouse City, the months passed and soon it was SUMMER. It was so hot, I could barely breathe!

I tried to **cool** myself down any way possible. I turned on two fans, put my feet in a bucket of **freezing** water, and put cold compresses on my head, but nothing helped! As my whiskers continued to sweat in the incredible heat, I daydreamed about going on vacation somewhere nice and cool, where I could be surrounded by **NATURE** instead of the **SWELTERING** concrete city.

Oh, what I would have given for the chance to dive into some cool ocean water. I would even settle for a nice **pool**!

As I was daydreaming, I went through

my **MAIL**. Mixed in with my regular mail was a *mysterious* envelope. **HOW STRANGE!** I opened it immediately. It was an invitation written on a piece of **crumpled** paper. It couldn't be from Uncle Stingysnout, could it?

Here's what it said:

THE HOTEL STINGYSNOUT IS PLEASED TO INVITE YOU AND YOUR FAMILY TO SPEND YOUR SUMMER VACATION WITH US (FOR FREE!). WE HAVE AIR-CONDITIONING, A BEAUTIFUL FLOWER GARDEN, AND A LOVELY POOL!

YOUR AFFECTIONATE UNCLE,

SAMUEL S. STINGYSNOUT

P.S. DON'T FORGET TO BRING YOUR BATHING SUIT!

I smiled, remembering all the work my family and I had done to help Uncle Stingysnout. And I was **HAPPY** that, at least for once, my uncle wasn't being thrifty. Instead, he had invited us to stay with him at his expense!

I called Trap, Thea, Benjamin, and even his friend Bugsy Wugsy! We packed our bags and headed straight to Hotel Stingysnout, where we had an extremely wonderful SUMMER VACATION. In the end, it's true that when you are kind and GENEROUS to others, that spirit of generosity is returned to you when you LEAST expect it!

# Be sure to read all my fabumouse adventures!

#1 Lost Treasure of the Emerald Eye

#2 The Curse of the Cheese Pyramid

#3 Cat and Mouse in a Haunted House

#4 I'm Too Fond of My Fur!

#5 Four Mice Deep in the Jungle

#6 Paws Off, Cheddarface!

#7 Red Pizzas for a Blue Count

#8 Attack of the Bandit Cats

#9 A Fabumouse Vacation for Geronimo

#10 All Because of a Cup of Coffee

#11 It's Halloween, You 'Fraidy Mouse!

#12 Merry Christmas, Geronimo!

#13 The Phantom of the Subway

#14 The Temple of the Ruby of Fire

#15 The Mona Mousa Code

#16 A Cheese-Colored Camper

#17 Watch Your Whiskers, Stilton!

#18 Shipwreck on the Pirate Islands

#19 My Name Is Stilton, Geronimo Stilton

#20 Surf's Up, Geronimo!

#21 The Wild, Wild
West

#22 The Secret
of Cacklefur Castle

A Christmas Tale

#23 Valentine's Day
Disaster

#24 Field Trip to
Niagara Falls

#25 The Search for
Sunken Treasure

#26 The Mummy
with No Name

#27 The Christmas
Toy Factory

#28 Wedding
Crasher

#29 Down and Out
Down Under

#30 The Mouse Island
Marathon

#31 The Mysterious
Cheese Thief

Christmas Catastrophe

#32 Valley of the
Giant Skeletons

#33 Geronimo and the
Gold Medal Mystery

#34 Geronimo Stilton,
Secret Agent

#35 A Very Merry
Christmas

#36 Geronimo's
Valentine

#37 The Race Across
America

#38 A Fabumouse
School Adventure

#39 Singing Sensation

#40 The Karate Mouse

#41 Mighty Mount
Kilimanjaro

#42 The Peculiar
Pumpkin Thief

#43 I'm Not a
Supermouse!

#44 The Giant
Diamond Robbery

#45 Save the White
Whale!

#46 The Haunted
Castle

#47 Run for the
Hills, Geronimo!

#48 The Mystery in
Venice

#49 The Way of
the Samurai

#50 This Hotel Is
Haunted

#51 The Enormouse
Pearl Heist

#52 Mouse in Space!

#53 Rumble in
the Jungle

#54 Get into Gear,
Stilton!

#55 The Golden
Statue Plot

#56 Flight of the
Red Bandit

The Hunt for the
Golden Book

#57 The Stinky
Cheese Vacation

# Up next!

#58 The Super
Chef Contest

# Don't miss these exciting Thea Sisters adventures!

**Thea Stilton and the Dragon's Code**

**Thea Stilton and the Mountain of Fire**

**Thea Stilton and the Ghost of the Shipwreck**

**Thea Stilton and the Secret City**

**Thea Stilton and the Mystery in Paris**

**Thea Stilton and the Cherry Blossom Adventure**

**Thea Stilton and the Star Castaways**

**Thea Stilton: Big Trouble in the Big Apple**

**Thea Stilton and the Ice Treasure**

**Thea Stilton and the Secret of the Old Castle**

**Thea Stilton and the Blue Scarab Hunt**

**Thea Stilton and the Prince's Emerald**

**Thea Stilton and the Mystery on the Orient Express**

**Thea Stilton and the Dancing Shadows**

**Thea Stilton and the Legend of the Fire Flowe**

**Thea Stilton and the Spanish Dance Mission**

**Thea Stilton and the Journey to the Lion's Den**

**Thea Stilton and the Great Tulip Heist**

**Thea Stilton and the Chocolate Sabotage**

Be sure to read all of our magical special edition adventures!

**THE KINGDOM OF FANTASY**

**THE QUEST FOR PARADISE:**
THE RETURN TO THE KINGDOM OF FANTASY

**THE AMAZING VOYAGE:**
THE THIRD ADVENTURE IN THE KINGDOM OF FANTASY

**THE DRAGON PROPHECY:**
THE FOURTH ADVENTURE IN THE KINGDOM OF FANTASY

**THE VOLCANO OF FIRE:**
THE FIFTH ADVENTURE IN THE KINGDOM OF FANTASY

**THEA STILTON: THE JOURNEY TO ATLANTIS**

**THEA STILTON: THE SECRET OF THE FAIRIES**

Join me and my friends on a journey through time in this very special edition!

THE JOURNEY
THROUGH TIME

# MEET GERONIMO STILTONIX

He is a spacemouse — the Geronimo Stilton of a parallel universe! He is captain of the spaceship *MouseStar 1*. While flying through the cosmos, he visits distant planets and meets crazy aliens. His adventures are out of this world!

#1 Alien Escape

#2 You're Mine, Captain!

# Meet
# GERONIMO STILTONOOT

He is a cavemouse — Geronimo Stilton's
ancient ancestor! He runs the stone
newspaper in the prehistoric village
of Old Mouse City. From dealing with
dinosaurs to dodging meteorites,
his life in the Stone Age is full
of adventure!

#1 The Stone of Fire

#2 Watch Your Tail!

#3 Help, I'm in Hot Lava!

#4 The Fast and
the Frozen

#5 The Great
Mouse Race

#6 Don't Wake the
Dinosaur!

# Meet
# CREEPELLA VON CACKLEFUR

I, *Geronimo Stilton*, have a lot of mouse friends, but none as **spooky** as my friend CREEPELLA VON CACKLEFUR! She is an enchanting and MYSTERIOUS mouse with a pet bat named **Bitewing**. YIKES! I'm a real 'fraidy mouse, but even I think CREEPELLA and her family are AWFULLY fascinating. I can't wait for you to read all about CREEPELLA in these a-mouse-ly funny and **spectacularly spooky** tales!

**#1 The Thirteen Ghosts**

**#2 Meet Me in Horrorwood**

**#3 Ghost Pirate Treasure**

**#4 Return of the Vampire**

**#5 Fright Night**

**#6 Ride for Your Life!**

# ABOUT THE AUTHOR

 Born in New Mouse City, Mouse Island, **GERONIMO STILTON** is Rattus Emeritus of Mousomorphic Literature and of Neo-Ratonic Comparative Philosophy. For the past twenty years, he has been running *The Rodent's Gazette*, New Mouse City's most widely read daily newspaper.

Stilton was awarded the Ratitzer Prize for his scoops on *The Curse of the Cheese Pyramid* and *The Search for Sunken Treasure*. He has also received the Andersen 2000 Prize for Personality of the Year. One of his bestsellers won the 2002 eBook Award for world's best ratlings' electronic book. His works have been published all over the globe.

In his spare time, Mr. Stilton collects antique cheese rinds and plays golf. But what he most enjoys is telling stories to his nephew Benjamin.

1. Main entrance
2. Printing presses (where the books and newspaper are printed)
3. Accounts department
4. Editorial room (where the editors, illustrators, and designers work)
5. Geronimo Stilton's office
6. Helicopter landing pad

THE RODENT'S GAZETTE

# Map of New Mouse City

1. Industrial Zone
2. Cheese Factories
3. Angorat International Airport
4. WRAT Radio and Television Station
5. Cheese Market
6. Fish Market
7. Town Hall
8. Snotnose Castle
9. The Seven Hills of Mouse Island
10. Mouse Central Station
11. Trade Center
12. Movie Theater
13. Gym
14. Catnegie Hall
15. Singing Stone Plaza
16. The Gouda Theater
17. Grand Hotel
18. Mouse General Hospital
19. Botanical Gardens
20. Cheap Junk for Less (Trap's store)
21. Aunt Sweetfur and Benjamin's House
22. Museum of Modern Art
23. University and Library
24. *The Daily Rat*
25. *The Rodent's Gazette*
26. Trap's House
27. Fashion District
28. The Mouse House Restaurant
29. Environmental Protection Center
30. Harbor Office
31. Mousidon Square Garden
32. Golf Course
33. Swimming Pool
34. Tennis Courts
35. Curlyfur Island Amusement Park
36. Geronimo's House
37. Historic District
38. Public Library
39. Shipyard
40. Thea's House
41. New Mouse Harbor
42. Luna Lighthouse
43. The Statue of Liberty
44. Hercule Poirat's Office
45. Petunia Pretty Paws's House
46. Grandfather William's House

Brigand's Isle

This way to the Rodent Straits

Pirate Ship
of Cats

Tomcat Island

Hamster Islands

Coral Reefs

This way
to the Mousific
Ocean

Blue Dolphin
Bay

Stray
Cat
Harbor

San Mouscisco

Cat's
Claw
Bay

Panther
Archipelag

Swissv

Cheddarton

Mouseport

This way
to the
Ratlantic Ocea

New Mouse City

Mousefort Beach

Furflung Island

N
W    E
S

This way to the Sea of Mice

MOUSE ISLAND

# Map of Mouse Island

Dear mouse friends,
Thanks for reading, and farewell
till the next book.
It'll be another whisker-licking-good
adventure, and that's a promise!

Geronimo Stilton

**Curse Of The Gloamglozer**

Stewart, Paul

| | | | |
|---|---|---|---|
| Reading Level: | 4.3 | Point Value: | 17.0 |
| Interest Level: | 3-5 | RC Quiz: | 37634 |